Agnes
and the Sheep

For Grandma, who loved her kinfolk
and made everything cosy ~ E.R.

For my Rose, Theo, & Toby ~ C.T.G.

Penguin Random House

Author Elle Rowley
Illustrator Clare Therese Gray

Editor Abi Luscombe
Senior Designer Elle Ward
Production Editor Dragana Puvacic
Production Controller Magdalena Bojko
Managing Editor Laura Gilbert
Special Sales and Custom Executive Issy Walsh
Publisher Francesca Young
Deputy Art Director Mabel Chan
Publishing Director Sarah Larter

First published in Great Britain in 2022 by
Dorling Kindersley Limited
DK, One Embassy Gardens, 8 Viaduct Gardens, London, SW11 7BW

The authorised representative in the EEA is
Dorling Kindersley Verlag GmbH. Arnulfstr. 124, 80636 Munich, Germany

Copyright © 2022 Dorling Kindersley Limited
A Penguin Random House Company
10 9 8 7 6 5 4 3 2 1
001–326763–Aug/2022

A CIP catalogue record for this book is available from the British Library.
ISBN: 978-0-2415-3610-0

Printed and bound in China

For the curious
www.dk.com

MIX
Paper | Supporting
responsible forestry
FSC™ C018179

This book was made with Forest Stewardship Council ™
certified paper – one small step in DK's commitment
to a sustainable future. For more information go to
www.dk.com/our-green-pledge

Agnes
and the Sheep

Written by
Elle Rowley

Illustrated by
Clare Therese Gray

On a little farm, behind a medium-sized cottage, lived a big dog named Agnes. She was strong, helpful, and wise (most of the time).

Agnes helped on the farm every day but there was nothing she loved more than being cosy.

Every night at exactly seven o'clock, she was allowed inside the cosy cottage to sleep in front of a cosy fire on a cosy bed and underneath a cosy blanket.

Agnes was not the only animal on the farm. There were many animals, including three sheep named Fern, Flax, and Baa Baa. The sheep loved the farm and were rather happy (most of the time).

They enjoyed morning walks with Agnes around the pasture and afternoon naps under the shade of their favourite tree. But, there was nothing that the sheep loved more than eating plants, especially green ones.

Plants were all they thought about, all they talked about, and even all they dreamed about. Their pasture was covered with plants so the sheep were really pleased.

Until, one day,
they weren't.

Fern, Flax, and Baa Baa always stayed in their pasture to graze, but one blustery afternoon they walked down the hill by the medium-sized cottage to escape the wind.

That's when they saw them.

Right through the windows of the cottage there they were:
PLANTS.

Plants hanging from the ceiling, shooting through the floor, and bursting from the bookshelves.

They were the brightest, greenest plants they had ever seen, much greener than the grass and plants in their own pasture. In fact, for the first time, the usually happy sheep felt quite unhappy and really hungry.

Meanwhile, Agnes realized the sheep had left their pasture. She quickly caught up with Fern, Flax, and Baa Baa to guide them back, but as she saw their eyes fixed on the cottage, she warned them.

"You cannot appreciate what you have got,
When you focus on what you have not."

Fern, Flax, and Baa Baa wanted to believe Agnes, so they returned to their pasture. But suddenly everything looked a little less green. And even tasted a little less green.

Not even the new spring grasses could entice them.

All they could think about, talk about, and even dream about was the cottage and the shiny, green plants **hanging** from the ceiling,

and plants **shooting** through the floor,

and plants **bursting** from the bookshelves.

One morning, the sheep and Agnes noticed
the family in the cottage loading up
their car with suitcases.

"Looks like I'll be looking after the cottage
tonight," Agnes said as they watched
the family drive away.

Fern, Flax, and
Baa Baa came up
with a plan.

That night, a few minutes before seven o'clock, the sheep left their pasture and quietly rolled down the hillside so as not to be heard by Agnes.

They watched behind a tree as Agnes put her nose under the door handle, lifted it up, and let herself right in.

When inside, she laid on her cosy bed, covered herself with her cosy blanket, and almost instantly fell into a deep, cosy sleep.

As Agnes dozed off, Fern, Flax, and Baa Baa
gently opened the door and tiptoed
right past her.

Once inside with the mouth-watering plants, the sheep agreed to eat just a small sample of each plant and then be on their way.

But each little bite led to a **bigger** bite, which led to...

...an unrestrained plant jamboree!

Then, quite suddenly, each of the sheep began to feel sick.

Very sick.

Baa Baa began to cry, "I will never eat someone else's greens again. I miss our pasture!"

Fern and Flax missed it, too. But they were so stuffed full they couldn't move a muscle.

Agnes, hearing Baa Baa's cries, finally awoke.
As she opened her mouth to scold the sheep for
making such a mess, she saw their miserable
faces and she knew she didn't need to.

Without a word, Agnes carefully carried the
sheep one by one back to their pasture, where
she laid each of them under their favourite tree.

The sheep were soon sleeping soundly, but Agnes slept
next to them, just to be sure they were all right.
Because if there was just one thing Agnes loved
more than being cosy, it was her friends.

When Fern, Flax, and Baa Baa awoke the next morning, the sheep realized that Agnes had been right. They had never been so happy to be on their pasture and they were sure that it had never looked so green.

Although it didn't quite matter anyway
because, for the first time ever,
they were not hungry.